THE
CAT
WHO
ATE
CHRISTMAS

With thanks to Freya

Copyright © 2016, 2018 by Hodder & Stoughton Limited
Illustrations © 2016, 2018 by Thomas Docherty

Running Press Kids
Hachette Book Group
1290 Avenue of the Americas, New York, NY 10104
www.runningpress.com/rpkids
@RP_Kids

Printed in China

Originally published in 2016 by Hodder & Stoughton Limited
(on behalf of its imprint Little, Brown Books for Young Readers) in the UK.

First U.S. Edition: October 2018

Published by Running Press Kids, an imprint of Perseus Books, LLC, a subsidiary of Hachette Book Group, Inc. The Running Press Kids name and logo is a trademark of the Hachette Book Group.

The Hachette Speakers Bureau provides a wide range of authors for speaking events. To find out more, go to www.hachettespeakersbureau.com or call (866) 376-6591.

The publisher is not responsible for websites (or their content) that are not owned by the publisher.

Print book cover and interior design by Sophie Burdess.

Library of Congress Control Number: 2017961784

ISBNs: 978-0-7624-6475-3 (hardcover), 978-0-7624-6477-7 (ebook)

1010

10 9 8 7 6 5 4 3 2 1

THE CAT WHO ATE CHRISTMAS

LIL CHASE & THOMAS DOCHERTY

RP|KIDS
PHILADELPHIA

It was Christmas Eve.

"Here, Jingles! Look nice for Santa."
Rose reached for the kitten and tried to tie
a piece of tinsel to his tail.

"*Yowl!*" Jingles didn't like anyone
touching his tail.

He sprang from the chair ... onto the
mantelpiece ... and right onto
the Christmas tree.

"*Meow!*"

The tree tilted, and the angel toppled. Jingles leapt to the floor, his paws skidding on a piece of wrapping paper.

"Oh, Jingles!" cried Lily as she caught the angel.

Jingles raced out of the room. Alex tried
to catch him, but his arms closed around thin
air. "Did you know that there are six hundred
million cats in the world?" he said. "But only
one as naughty as Jingles!"

"Quick! Before Mom and Dad see."
Lily *heeeeeaved* the tree upright. *Oof!*
They hung up the decorations again.

"Mom spent lots of time making these,"
said Alex, as he smoothed out the bent
corners of a tinfoil star.

Lily straightened the angel's dress.
"Now they're as good as new."

"Time to hang
up your stockings!"
Dad called from
the kitchen.

"Should we leave a treat for the reindeer?" asked Lily.

"Reindeer like carrots," Alex told them.

"Jingles needs a treat," said Rose.

"Now, into your PJs. Quick!" said Mom, as she chased them upstairs.

Pajamas on.

Teeth brushed.

Teeth checked.

Teeth brushed again.

Into bed!

15

"I hope Santa Claus brings me new ballet shoes," said Lily.

"I want a book of fascinating facts!" said Alex.

"I want to cuddle Jingles," said Rose.

"Did you know," yawned Alex, "that the tallest Christmas tree was over two-hundred feet tall?"

Dad ruffled Alex's hair. "Did *you* know
that if you're not asleep when Santa Claus
arrives he won't leave you anything?"

Alex squeezed his eyes shut tight.

"If you see Santa Claus," said Mom, as she turned out the light, "please say 'Merry Christmas' from me."

Then Alex, Lily, and Rose were each given . . .

a kiss

and a hug

and a look that said, *Go to sleep now.*

Mom scooped up Jingles and left the
bedroom, pulling the door almost shut.

"Good night," Rose murmured.

"Good . . ." Lily began to say, but the rest of her words fell away.

If Lily had still been
awake, she would have
seen . . .

. . . that a visitor had
arrived!

The next morning, the children ran into their parents' room.

"It's **CHRISTMAS DAY!**"

"Time to get up!"

Dad rubbed his eyes. "It's five-thirty in the morning," he said, yawning.

"It's ten-thirty in India," Alex said. "Come on!"

One step, two steps, three steps . . .

      they crept down the stairs.

Then Lily snapped on a light and . . .

They froze.

"What . . . ?" asked Lily.

"When . . . ?" whispered Alex.

"How . . . ?" said Dad, peering over the tops of their heads.

Jingles leapt from Rose's arms.

"All your lovely decorations," said Lily, taking her mom's hand.

The family followed Jingles into the living room.

"The presents are all unwrapped!"
said Alex, stepping over a pile of crumpled
wrapping paper.

"*Meow!*"

Jingles was at the top
of the Christmas tree. He
didn't look happy at all.

Rose took a big breath.
Dad tried to get to her but—

**"WAHHHHHHHH!
JINGLES BROKE
CHRISTMAS."**

Jingles winced. His fur stood up on end and then . . .

Creeeeeeak.

CRASH!

The tree collapsed into a heap of glitter
and tinsel.

"Oh, Jingles!" cried Mom.

How had one little kitten done all this?

"What a naughty cat," Dad said to Mom, looking at the decorations Mom had spent so long making.

"Naughty cat!" said Rose.

"I can fix them," said Mom. "You go and find Jingles. Tell him I'm not mad," she added. "Not really."

Jingles was hiding under the bed.

The children waved Jingles's favorite things at him.

"Here, little kitten," said Alex.

"We're not mad," said Lily. "Not really."

But Jingles didn't want to come out.

"Jingles will come out when he's ready," said Mom.

"Cocoa," said Dad. "The fix for everything. Even a broken Christmas."

After breakfast, Lily, Alex, and Rose played with their presents. Everyone forgot how naughty Jingles had been.

Mom whistled as she took the turkey out
of the oven. Dad hummed as he set the table.
  "There. Christmas is perfect again,"
said Dad.

"Let's go and get Grandma," said Mom.

"Yay!" The children jumped up.

Mom bundled Rose into a scarf while Lily pulled on her new winter hat and Alex climbed into his boots.

"Where's Jingles?" asked Dad. "We
don't want him ruining your decorations
again, honey."

"Naughty cat!" said Rose.

"I'll make sure he's upstairs," said Lily.

Jingles was still hiding.

"We're going to get Grandma, Jingles," Lily told him. "We'll be back in time for lunch."

"Come on, Lily!" called Dad's voice.

"You stay here, out of trouble," she told
Jingles. Then she jumped to her feet and
ran downstairs, quickly shutting the bedroom
door behind her.

Too quickly . . .

DEEEEEELICIOUS!

CREEEEEEAK . . .

SNIFF . . .

It didn't take long to get to Grandma's house, even through the snow.

The children couldn't wait to tell her all about their presents.

"How's Jingles?" Grandma asked Mom.

"He's under the bed," said Alex. "In disgrace."

"He ruined Mom's decorations," Lily explained.

"He's a naughty cat," added Rose.

"He's . . . Jingles," Mom said with a sigh.

Everyone was really hungry when they got back from Grandma's.

"I can't wait to eat Mom's special Christmas turkey," said Dad.

"*Deeelicious,*" said Rose.

Dad opened the back door, stepped into the kitchen, and ...

. . . slid across the floor.

"ARGHHHH!"

"What . . . ?" asked Grandma.

"When . . . ?" whispered Alex.

"How . . . ?" wondered Lily.

"Jingles!" said Mom. "You ate my TURKEY!"

Rose's bottom lip quivered.

"Jingles was very hungry," said Lily,
throwing chewed parsnips into the bin.

"Jingles was very lucky," said Grandma, picking up what was left of the turkey.

"Jingles was very naughty," said Rose.

"Where *is* Jingles?" asked Alex.

They all went outside to look for their naughty kitten.

"I think he ran away because we shouted," said Lily, in a worried voice.

"I wasn't really mad at Jingles," said Mom.
"Not *really*."

"I want Jingles!" said Rose.

"We'll find him," said Dad. "Come on."

They went and asked the neighbors. No Jingles.

They kept looking,

56

and walking,

and looking,

all the way into town.

No Jingles.

"Jingles doesn't like singing,"
said Alex. "He especially doesn't
like Rose's singing."

Lily twisted her braids. She did
that when she was worried.

They went to the park.
No Jingles.
"This is no good!" cried Lily,
chewing her braids.
Jingles was happiest when
he was at home. That was where he
should be.

"Maybe he'll come home all by himself,"
said Mom.

"Come on," said Grandma. "It's getting
dark. Let's head back. You can drop me off
on the way."

But when they got home, the house was empty.

"Jingles has never run away from home before," said Alex.

"He'll be all right," said Dad.

"I wonder what he's doing," said Lily.

"I'm sure he's having fun!" said Mom.

That night, everyone dreamed of Jingles.

The next morning, Lily and Alex didn't want any breakfast.

"Jingles loves breakfast," said Lily.

"We should fill his bowl as usual," said Alex. "Then maybe he'll come home."

Rose stood on her tiptoes and opened the cupboard.

"No cat food!" she cried.

Alex, Lily, and Rose ran to Mom and Dad.
"Come on! Come on! We need to go to the
supermarket. RIGHT NOW!"

There wasn't even time to get dressed.

When they got to the supermarket, they ran into Grandma coming in to work.

"What a nice surprise!" Grandma said, hugging them. "What are you doing here?"

"We ran out of food for Jingles," said Alex.

"We need to buy more so he'll come home,"
said Lily.

PET FOOD →

It took forever to get to the pet food aisle, because everyone kept stopping to say "Merry Christmas!"

Jingles's favorite turkey treats were on the top shelf.

Alex, Lily, and Rose reached up to get them.

Mom and Dad came to help.

"What else would Jingles like?"
asked Mom.

Lily chose a bright red collar.

Alex picked a
scratching post.

Rose wanted a toy mouse.

"He'll definitely come home when he hears
this!" Lily shook the bag of treats.

They went to the checkout to pay for everything, daydreaming about their kitten coming home.

Beep! Beep! Beep! Beep! "**MEOW!**"

"Jingles! You came back!"

"A cat?!" said the man behind the register.

"Our kitten ran away," Alex explained.

"Naughty cat," said Rose.

"Where have you been?" Lily asked.

Grandma suddenly guessed where Jingles
had been hiding. (Can you?)

Mom paid. Dad packed the bags.
It was time to take Jingles home.

Back at home, they played with
Jingles and his new toys until it
was time for bed.

Pajamas on.

Teeth brushed.

Teeth checked.

Perfect!

Jingles made himself comfy on Lily's pillow. She sighed, smiling as she gazed up at the skylight.

"Did you see . . . ?" asked Alex.

"I did!" said Lily.

"Santa Claus!" gasped Rose.

"Maybe he didn't want to leave until he knew Jingles was safe," wondered Lily.

"Until he knew we had everything we wanted for Christmas," Alex said.

"Go to sleep now," said Mom, with her serious look. But she wasn't mad, not really.

"Jingles ate Christmas," said Rose. Everyone laughed.

"He did," said Mom. "But we'll always love him."

As the bedroom door closed, Lily's eyelids grew heavy. It had been a long day.

"Good night," murmured Alex.

"Night, night," said Rose.

"We love you, Jingles," said Lily, reaching out to stroke their cat. Her hand closed around thin air. Her eyes snapped open. "Where's . . ."

ALEX'S
CHRISTMAS FACTS

Alex loves facts. Here are some of his favorite facts about Christmas—and cats!

The tallest Christmas tree was displayed in 1950 at the Northgate Shopping Center in Seattle, Washington. It was 221 feet tall!

Cats can hear better than dogs—and humans!

Santa has nine reindeer. Their names are
Dasher, Dancer, Prancer, Vixen, Comet, Cupid,
Donner, and Blitzen—and of course Rudolph,
who leads the way with
his glowing red nose.

Where do you leave your stocking for Santa?
In some countries, children don't have a
Christmas stocking! In France, Germany,
Mexico, and Iceland, children put their shoes
by the window or under the Christmas tree to
be filled with presents.

In North and Northwest India, Christmas Day
is known as Bada Din, which means "Big Day."

Cats love to sleep. In fact, they spend
about two-thirds of their whole
life sleeping! Zzzz . . .

Has your cat ever eaten
your turkey? If you lived in
Poland or Slovakia, you'd be eating a fish
called carp for Christmas dinner!

 The world record for
the fastest time to decorate a Christmas tree
is held by Sharon Juantuah from Essex,
United Kingdom. She decorated her tree in
just 36.89 seconds!

A male cat is called a tom,
and a female cat is called
a queen or a molly.

CHRISTMAS CRACKER JOKES

Q. What do you get if you cross Santa with a duck?

A. A Christmas quacker!

Q. What is Santa Claus's dog called?

A. Santa Paws!

Q. What do you get if you cross a Christmas bell with a skunk?

A. Jingle Smells!

Oh, oh, oh !

Q. What goes "Oh, oh, oh"?
A. Santa walking backwards!

Q. Why did the turkey cross the road?
A. Because it was the chicken's day off!

Q. Who hides in the bakery at Christmas?
A. Mince spies!

Q. What did one snowman say to the other snowman?
A. I can smell carrots!

HOW TO MAKE COCOA

Dad made cocoa to cheer everyone up after Jingles caused chaos! Here's the recipe so you can enjoy it, too. You will need a grownup to help you.

INGREDIENTS:

2 cups of milk

1 tablespoon of powdered sugar

2 tablespoons of cocoa powder

2 oz dark chocolate, finely grated
(ask a grownup to do this for you!)

½ teaspoon ground cinnamon (optional)

Whipped cream, marshmallows, sprinkles
(optional, for decorating)

INSTRUCTIONS:

1. Pour the milk into a
large saucepan. Ask a grownup to
turn the heat up to medium and wait until it is
simmering gently (not boiling).

2. Add the powdered sugar, cocoa powder,
grated chocolate, and cinnamon. With the pan
still on the burner, whisk for a couple minutes
until all the ingredients are mixed.

3. Ask a grownup to carefully pour the
hot cocoa into mugs. Add whipped cream,
marshmallows, and sprinkles to decorate, if
you want.

4. Drink your cocoa and try not
to get a chocolate moustache!

HOW TO MAKE
A CHRISTMAS ANGEL

In the story, Mom is an artist and has made
lots of beautiful Christmas decorations.
Here's how you can make your own
Christmas angel to go on top of your tree.

YOU WILL NEED:

- A toilet paper roll

- Stiff paper (for the angel's wings—any color you like)

- Wool, string or strips of fabric, or paper (for the angel's hair—any color you like)

- Colored pens, pencils, or paint

- Child-friendly scissors

- A glue stick

- Any decorations that you like! You could use sequins, stickers, tinsel, feathers, shapes cut out of colored paper or fabric, etc.

- Our template for the angel's wings (p.95). You can trace it or ask a grownup to photocopy it for you.

INSTRUCTIONS:

1. Use the template on the next page to draw the outline of the angel's wings on your stiff paper. Cut out and decorate as you like. If you have feathers, you could glue them on!

2. Glue the wings on to the back of the toilet paper roll as seen in the picture here.

3. Glue the angel's hair on to the top of the tube as in the picture below. Leave room for her face!

4. Draw the angel's face. You can also decorate the rest of the roll with your colored pens, pencils, or paint, and any decorations you have.

5. When the glue is dry, you can ask a grownup to place your angel on top of the Christmas tree.

ABOUT THE AUTHOR

Lil Chase lives in London with her husband and daughter. Having been a bar cook and even suffered a brief stint in Disneyland Paris, she settled on a career in her first love—telling stories. Visit her online at www.lilchase.com.

ABOUT THE ILLUSTRATOR

Thomas Docherty is an acclaimed author and illustrator of children's picture books, including *Little Boat, Big Scary Monster, The Driftwood Ball,* and Jenny Colgan's Polly and the Puffin series. *The Snatchabook,* which was written by his wife Helen, has been shortlisted for several awards in the UK and US and has been translated into 17 languages.

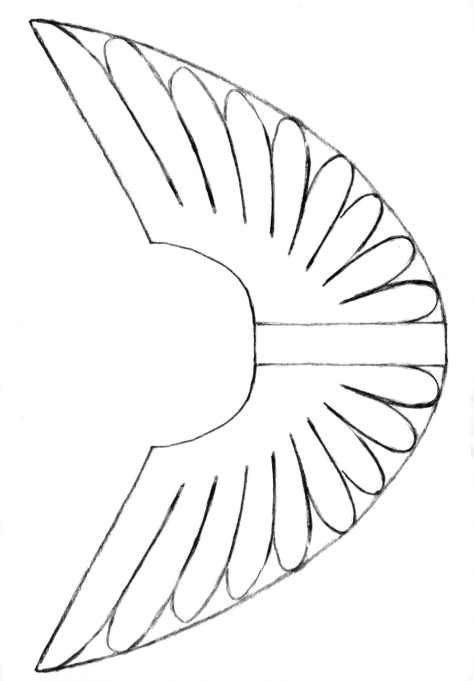

CONGRATULATIONS!

Congratulations to Millie from Fairways Primary School, who won the competition to name the kitten in this book with her suggestion of "Jingles." A big thank you to Millie, and to all the children who entered the competition, which was hosted by Lovereading4kids.co.uk.